DRAGONS' WOOD
D0258640

DRAGONS' WOOD

BY
BRIAN MOSES

ILLUSTRATED BY
ED BOXALL

Published by TROIKA

First published 2019

Troika Books Ltd
Well House, Green Lane, Ardleigh CO7 7PD
www.troikabooks.com

A CIP catalogue record for this book is available from the British Library

ISBN 978-1-912745-08-1

1 3 5 7 9 10 8 6 4 2

Printed in India

For little dragons, Willow & Ruby

BRIAN

For Flynn, Sammy, Rachel,
Dixie and Hastings Woodcraft Folk

ED

and all dragons – wherever
they hide

We didn't see dragons
in Dragons' Wood

but we saw
where the dragons had been...

As we twisted between the trees
we saw tracks in soft mud

that could only have been scratched
by some sharp clawed creature.

As we lifted the leaves
we saw scorched earth
where heat from a dragon's roar
had whitened everything to ash.

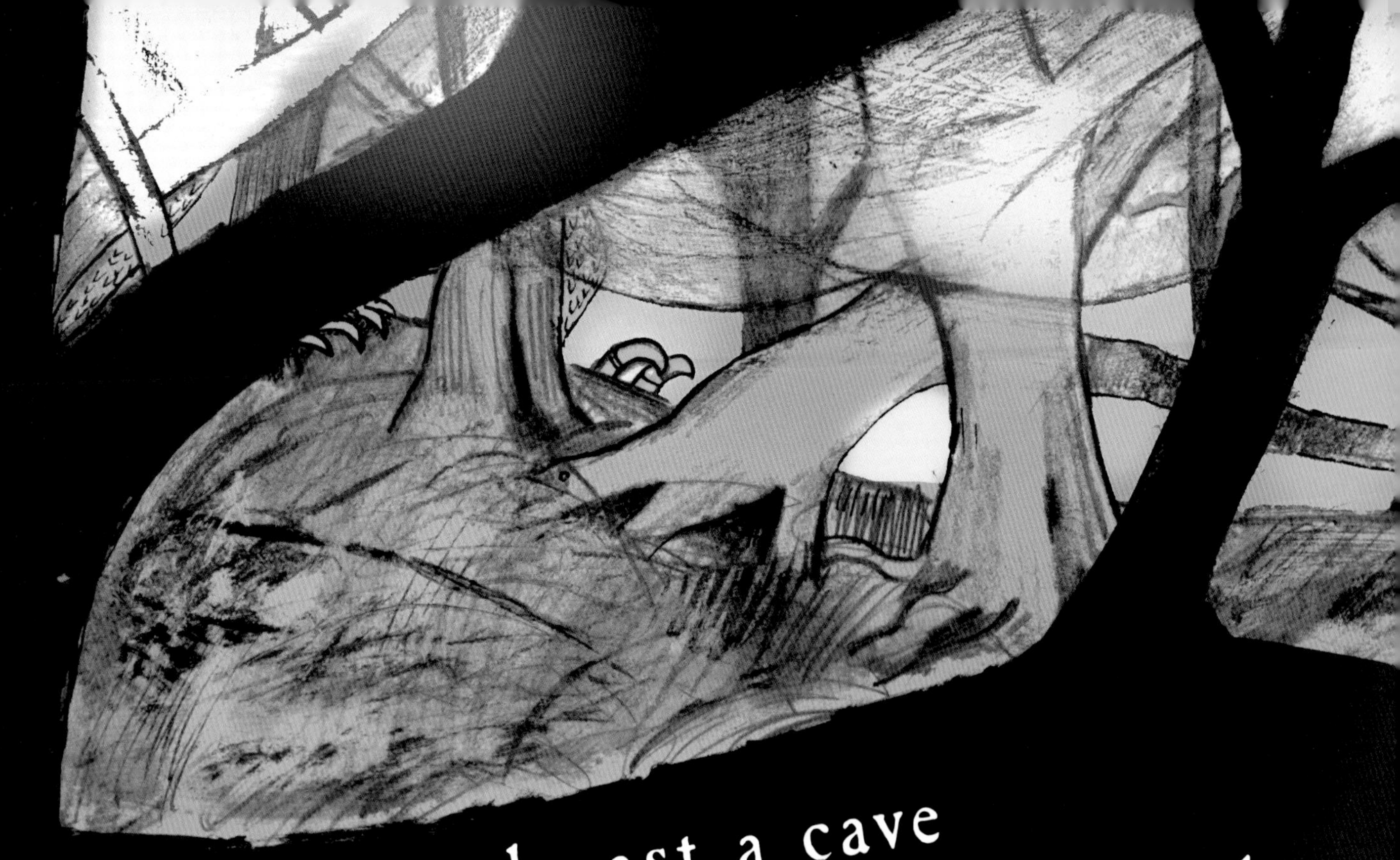

As we hurried past a cave
we saw mist like the smoky breath

from some sleeping creature within.

As we gazed into a pool

we saw the shimmering scales
of a dragon's shed skin.

As we looked inside a hollow trunk
we saw the bones

from a dragon's latest feast.

As we ducked beneath low-hanging branches

we saw dragon dung rolled into boulders.

As we stumbled along the path
we saw dragon eggs, half-hidden

among the fallen leaves.

As we sat beside a waterfall

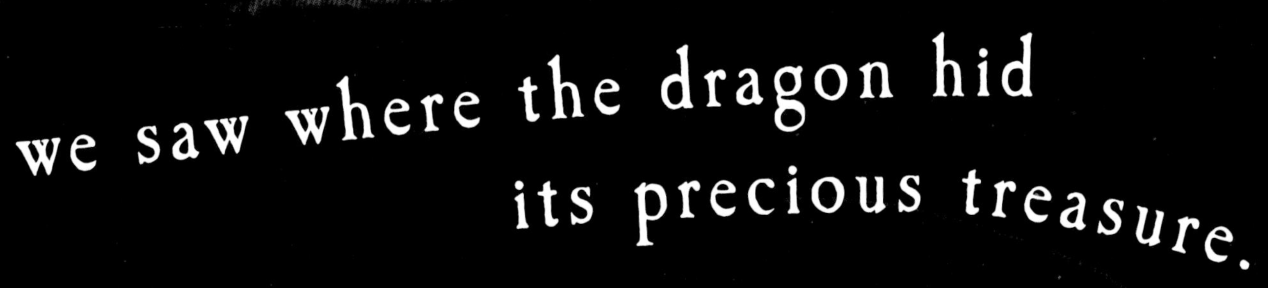

we saw where the dragon hid
its precious treasure.

As we turned for home
we saw above us
the sky streaked with flame.

We didn't see dragons
in Dragons' Wood,
but this was the closest
we'd ever been...

to believing.

DRAGONS'
WOOD

DRAGONS'
WOOD

DRAGONS'
WOOD

DRAGONS'
WOOD

ABOUT THE AUTHOR

BRIAN MOSES has been a professional children's poet since 1988. He has had over 200 books published including *Lost Magic* and *The Monster Sale* and edited anthologies such as *The Secret Lives of Teachers* and *Aliens Stole My Underpants*.

His books for Troika are *Beetle in the Bathroom*, *I Thought I Heard a Tree Sneeze: The very best of Brian Moses' Poems for Young Children* and *Walking with My Iguana*.

Brian also runs writing workshops and performs his own poetry and percussion shows. He has given over 3000 performances in schools, libraries, theatres and at festivals in UK and abroad. Brian is co-director of a nationwide able writers' administered by Authors Abroad.

To find out more about Brian visit his website: www.brianmoses.co.uk

ABOUT THE ILLUSTRATOR

ED BOXALL is a childrens' poet, illustrator, musician, educator and performer. He has written and illustrated many books, such as *Mr Trim and Miss Jumble* for Walker Books and *High In The Old Oak Tree* for his own Pearbox Press. His first collection *Me and My Alien Friend: Cosmic Poems About Friendship* is published by Troika. He has also illustrated *Walking with My Iguana* by Brian Moses.

Ed performs his poems with a mix of spoken word, projections at schools, art centres and festivals. He lives in Hastings, a small town on the south coast of England.

To find out more about Ed visit his website: www.edboxall.com